For Louisa —BB

For Worth, Adlai, and Alouette —EB

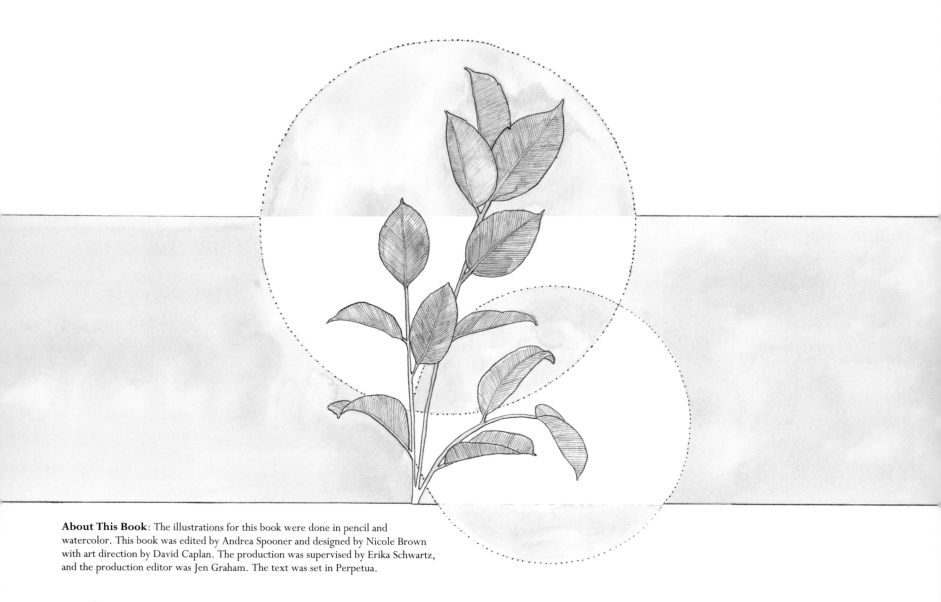

About This Book: The illustrations for this book were done in pencil and watercolor. This book was edited by Andrea Spooner and designed by Nicole Brown with art direction by David Caplan. The production was supervised by Erika Schwartz, and the production editor was Jen Graham. The text was set in Perpetua.

Being Edie

Is Hard Today

Written by BEN BRASHARES

Illustrated by ELIZABETH BERGELAND

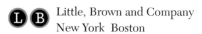 Little, Brown and Company
New York Boston

Being Edie was hard today.
She barely made it to breakfast.
"Please eat your toast, Edie," her mom said.
"I'm too tired to eat my toast," Edie replied.
"Please sit up, Edie," her mom said.
"I can't," Edie said. "My head is too heavy."

"Pony or piggy?" her mom asked while
they waited for the school bus.
"Piggy, please, Mother," Edie answered.
When the bus arrived, Edie reminded her
mother that piggies don't go to school.
"This little piggy does," her mom said,
and scooted Edie out the door.

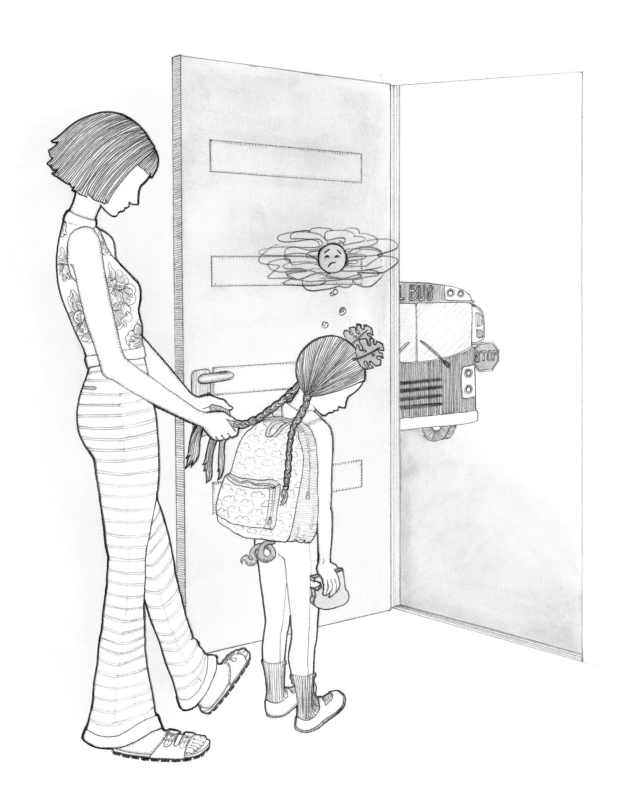

She had made a mistake. A pony
would have been much better.

While putting her things away,
Edie thought for a moment about
climbing into her cubby.
Maybe just hanging there.
Like a bat.
Until it was time to go home.

In class, Ms. Meany called on Edie to write on the board, but Edie didn't know the answer.

"I can't," she said.
"Why can't you, Edie?"
"I have polar bear hands,"
she said, and showed her.

At recess, Edie sat in her favorite spot and ate her favorite snack (sardines).

"Only squids eat sardines," one boy said.

"Edie, the stinky squid!" they sang. "EE-dee-the-STINK—ee-SQUID!"

And they circled her like sharks.

Oh, to be a squid.

Alone, she sat on the swing where she'd go to think
and imagine she had great wings that could take her high above.
But the wings never worked.

So she decided to be a cheetah,
the fastest, fiercest land animal on earth.

Her stomach grumbled.

The lunch bell rang.

And she was off.

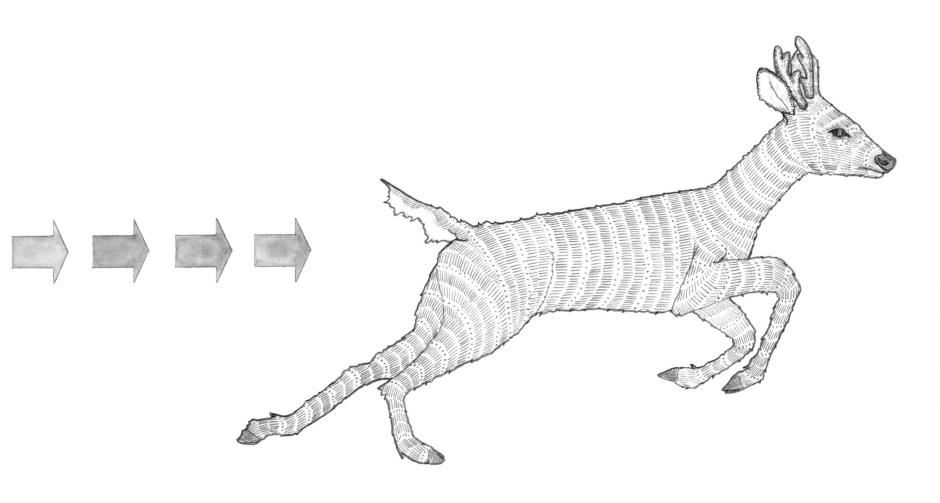

During her rather long trip to the principal's office, Edie tried to explain the slow-moving characteristics of a sloth, but Ms. Meany wasn't listening.

Edie figured if she just. Sat. Still enough....
the principal probably wouldn't see her.

"Edie. Edie. Edie? Eeeeeeeedeeeeeeee!"

Chameleon was definitely the right choice.

For the ride home,
Edie considered a porcupine
or a hissing cockroach.
Eventually she decided to be an armadillo.

But inside, she felt like a naked mole rat.

At dinner, Edie was lost in thought.

"Edie, would you like to use your fork?" her mom asked.

"No, thank you, Mother. This is how butterflies taste their food."

When it was time for bed, Edie found that she had,
unfortunately, become a worm.
"EDIE! 'EASE come 'rush your teesh!"

"I can't!
I don't have teeth!
Or hands, even!"

"Honey, come pick out your clothes for school tomorrow,"
Edie's mom called from the other room.
"Worms don't go to school!" Edie yelled back.

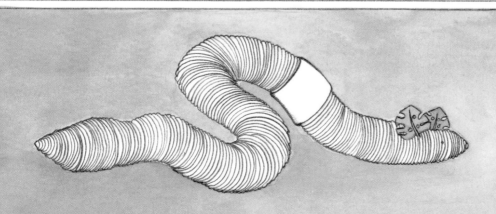

But her mom didn't hear her.
Because people can't hear worms.

The floor was uncomfortable, so Edie found
her feet and pulled herself up to the mirror.
She hoped to see something new.

But she only saw Edie.
Edie, who had to go to school tomorrow.

Edie sat on her bed and held her knees as tears filled her eyes.

"Mom?" she said. "I don't think I want to go to school tomorrow."

Just saying the words made the tears jump out.

Her mom stroked her arm and let her cry.

"Did you know," her mom finally said, reaching out to collect
a tear, "that humans are the only creatures on earth that cry
tears when they're sad? And no one really knows why."
Edie looked up and wiped her eyes. "I think *I* do. It's just like
why the sky cries when it's sad," she said.

"I learned about it in school," Edie went on. "The clouds get dark and fill up with tears and then, when the clouds can't hold any more, the tears fall all the way down to the ground, where they help make flowers grow and make streams for animals to drink out of and take baths in…."
Edie's mom smiled. "So…does the sky feel better after it cries?"

"Oh yeah," Edie said. "The clouds get all fluffy again, and the sun comes out."

"You feeling a little fluffier?" her mom asked, pulling her in for a hug.

"Yeah. I guess. Like a fluffy baby owl. Owls are nocturnal, you know,
so I'm going to stay up all—"

"Night night, Edie."

"Pony or piggy?" her mom asked the next morning.

"Piggy, please, Mother," Edie replied. "No, wait—pony!"

"You sure?" her mom asked.

"Pony *and* piggy…and anteater, frog, lemur, lion, hedgehog, and…flying squirrel."

"Okay, but no cheetahs today." Her mom kissed the top of her head. "Better yet, how about you just go as my favorite little girl Edie?"

Edie thought for a moment.

"Yeah, okay. I guess being
Edie's pretty good, too."